THE CLAN OF MUNES

MW00860813

THE CLAN OF MUNES

BY

FREDERICK J. WAUGH, N.A.

COACHWHIP PUBLICATIONS

Greenville, Ohio

For more vintage titles of
fantasy, mystery, fright,
fun, and adventure,
visit CoachwhipBooks.com.

The Clan of Munes, by Frederick J. Waugh
© 2023 Coachwhip Publications edition

First published 1916
Frederick Judd Waugh, 1861-1940
CoachwhipBooks.com

ISBN 1-61646-548-4
ISBN-13 978-1-61646-548-3

Frederick J. Waugh was an American illustrator
and seascape artist. His interest in fairy tales and
the supernatural led to the creation of *The Clan
of Munes,* which he hoped would develop further
as an American fairy tale. Unfortunately, sales
were slow, and he bought back many of the printed copies, so they are scarce today.

THE CLAN OF MUNES

THE munes? Why, their name is legion; everywhere you go upon their island you see differences; no two are alike; they are as different as a half and a quarter. From whence came they and whither are they going? What are they for and why do they resemble old spruce roots and stumps and odds and ends of rotten wood?

You may ask me all these questions and I shall try to answer them. For once upon a time a big bubble of gas under the crust of the earth, where the sea was fifty fathoms deep, exploded with such violence that it heaved up all the rocks and sand from the bottom, and after awhile the birds came and dropped seeds and left them upon the sands, and because there was much rotted seaweed in the sand the seeds took root, and by and by the dust of the air settled along with these first seedlings, and gradually it came about that the soil thus formed was stronger and more seeds grew; and the birds also brought seeds from spruce cones, and spruce-trees grew until they became so old that many of them fell into a state of decay; others were torn and broken by storms, riven by lightning, and eaten by ants until their broken limbs dropped from their sockets: and these were the first mune caps, or hats, if you like that better.

Then after awhile came a clever little wizard from the north with a great collection of ancient Indian finery in which he often arrayed himself after he had painted his face in bright colors. He had been trying for some time to prevail upon the magic, in which he seemed to be well versed, to change him from an ordinary little wizard, who could make some things appear and most things disappear, into a great Indian magician. Whether of the Tlingit, Haida, or other Indian clan it mattered little so long as he could dress up in his Indian finery to some purpose. One day when he was in the midst of an incantation he happened to see lying upon the ground near him several butt ends of limbs and branches which had fallen from their sockets in a near-by spruce stump, and he noted their wonderful resemblance to certain tall hats and caps of a new and original pattern. "Now," said he, "as I have by me many more totems than I can manage to use myself, I will make me a clan the like of which has never before been seen. These extra totems will I give their families so that we shall be a people great and strong and well tried out and weather-tested, for my clan shall be of seasoned wood, of spruce created and constructed and put together by my magic and my set of Indian tools whereof I have reason to be proud."

SO the wizard forthwith set about to gather together all the odds and ends of the sculptured remains of ancient spruce-trees, and arranged an open-air workshop in that part of the island the most accessible to his needs and wants. Here he set up various totem-poles to aid him in this new and great and glorious work of making unto himself a people. He also fashioned himself a house after the manner of the northern Indian clans, with a great totem-pole in front and a round hole for a front door. Many dark and mysterious matters worked out to decorate its interior and to make him comfortable, as a wizard should be under high pressure of work.

So the wizard cunningly joined together these fragments of spruce-trees until he had made him several little wooden images. Two of them he recognized at once as looking very much like Adam and Eve, while the rest were just runes. But it did not matter much which was Adam and which was Eve, for, no doubt, to everyone except the wizard they all seemed very much alike.

Now, when he found that he had put together most of the clan of runes, he was struck with the necessity of giving them life so that they could move about and talk. He got out his medicine-chest, for he was also well versed in the science of herbs and mixed together strong potions of balsam and juniper and cranberry and sweet-fern and other acrid and resinous magic ingredients. He made over them incantations in which all the totems joined, especially the totem rattles, who rattled furiously until he was forced to tell them to stop their racket, the only difference being the magic way in which he told them to do so, for they were all his obedient servants and did what he told him to furnish them with rune families, which no good little self-respecting totem could do without.

ALL being then in readiness, the potions soon to boil and the totems quiet and all stirring hard at the hops of newly made runes, the wizard poured over them all the liquid, unctuous, spicy stuff which he had brewed, until they were well soaked, all their cracks and crevices filled, and they were softened and well seasoned in the elixir. When this was finished winter had set in and the first snow had fallen and it was very deep; and because of its deepness the wizard dug holes in it and laid within each hole a newly created

rune, all running and streaming at the pores with liquid fragrance. He stuck a totem rattle beside each snowy, cold-storage chamber, to guard its rune while the winter cold should do its work, and he turned in to hibernate in his own house upon the hill until spring.

And so the totems out in the winter wind had to rattle continuously all the winter to keep from freezing, but the wild runes froze and froze as the winter grew darker and blacker and colder; and wherever the balsam lay between their joined parts it hardened and toughened in the silent chill until veins were formed. In the spring came a great thaw and the woods melted together as in one piece and a great, tough softness was established throughout their entire bodies. And, although the outer, sharper parts of them were more or less hard, yet they were all well locked together by tendons and sinews and ligaments. They resembled the construction of the hippopotamus, the rhinoceros, the armadillo, and all of the armored fishes in that although hard and tough they were yet flexible enough to move about very quickly.

At last, when most of the snow had melted and the totems began to feel the winter chill fading away and giving place to the genial warmth of spring, all the runes awoke and sat up one after another and stretched and yawned and looked about for something to eat. They were all very hungry; and the totems all rattled with great joy thinking that now had they each found the head of a family to which they would be good little totems forever. But, alas, here the power of the totems seemed to end, no mune caring any more for totem rattles or for totem-poles or any other totem junk than did the old spruce stumps from which the clan had sprung.

UT the wizard succeeded at that time in producing only one mune with eyes like humans which could see far and near, round and flat as well. All of the others had eyes which were flat like spectacles and shone like mother-of-pearl. It is very certain that they could see, but in some mysterious way different from the single mune with the human eyes; and they saw at night, too, as well as day, for they never stopped in their stunts day or night—apparently they never slept. And the wizard said: "I see that I have made something very strange and amusing; now I shall teach them manners and customs.

WHEN they get together at the close of day I shall teach them to gossip, and when they are all at it good and strong then will I spy upon them from my hiding-place; for unless I find out what they are driving at I shall never be able, with all my wisdom, to understand the stealthy cunning of their ways. But never shall they see me or the sunset, because that would not be good magic." At which speech all the totems rattled, thinking that now the time had really come when the mines could be persuaded to leave their most mysterious ways and be good little totem-ridden mines. But we shall see. So the wizard, continuing, said :

"I WILL give them a bird—he shall first appear reclining upon an old spruce stump, and when they have walked round him ten times he will split up into ten birds; and because he is a fire-bird I shall command them to call him and his kind torch-birds. And the torch-birds shall fly continually within and without the great, hot oven between the stumps at Dead Man's Cove, fanning the flames which by my magic I have set there in the midst, continually to burn.

"AND this is where immunes who fear fire shall become immune to it by being well and seasonably burned within these sacred precincts, and by their screams all immunes shall know that they are forever immune, and without the gate which leads into this fiery pit shall watch a party of immunes who at the crucial moment shall snatch, as it were, the brand from the burning 'and save the new immune from an ashen grave.

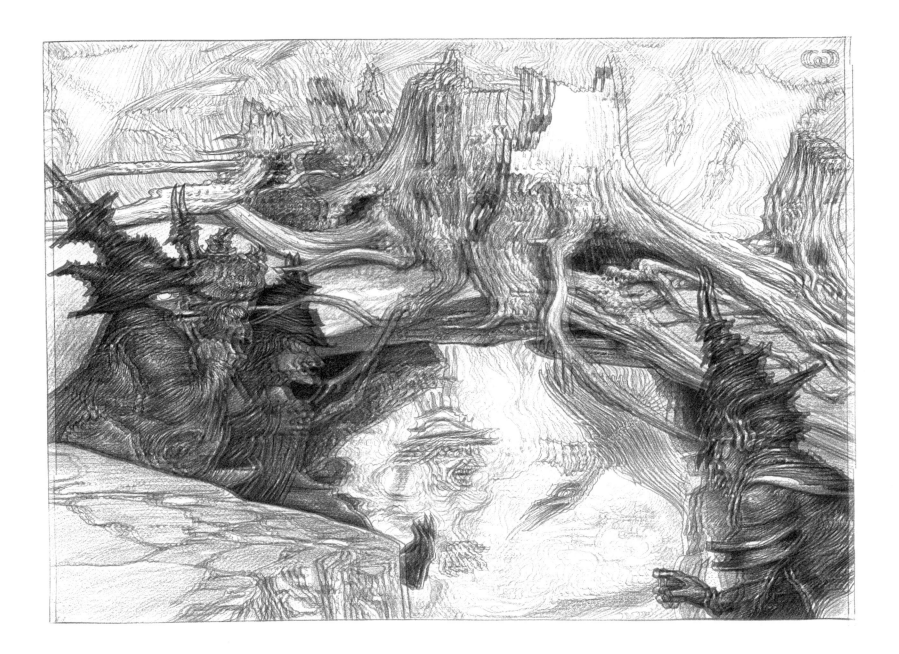

"ND if it shall come to pass that any of my munes shall quarrel among themselves, I shall take unto myself a dog from the roots and stumps of ancient spruce, and this dog shall hold himself in readiness to settle all quarrels, and as they wax hotter and hotter in their disputes and brandish their swords and spears and clubs in threatening fury,——

"AND when one is about to slay another, and when the other is under the sword, then shall the dog which I have by my magic created be set upon the fallen foe, perchance to bite him until, maddened, he gains strength to rise again; and he who pulls off the dog shall be the lifelong mate of him from whom the dog was pulled.

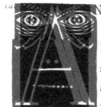

"AND he who has the seeing eyes shall sit upon his throne, for I have made him king. And unto him have I given ministers, four or five, to thump and scrape and pipe to him, day in and day out, for to keep him quiet as a good king should be, lest he become ambitious and usurp the world.

"AND it is given unto the king to see his subjects sometimes here and sometimes there, but mostly there, especially near the Wild Rocks, in full sight of the Old Man Rock afar, some rods or more from off the shore, where, uprising from the toss and tumble of the surf, rise wraiths of mist likewise created of my magic, and these do beckon anon and anon those watched munes who, all unknowing of their fate, approach the forbidden coast and there headlong to fall into the sea. Many of them will be dashed hither and yon among the wild, wet, seaweeded rocks and all their rougher parts ground among the cobbles, until, for aught I know, they might as well be mites of driftwood, so little will they resemble their former selves.

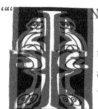IN this condition oftentimes I see them floating out upon the surface of the sea, whereupon a strong desire to hear what they are saying possesses me, and, hiding them within my great canoe, I approach them stealthily upon the waves. And yet that which they say to one another puzzles me; it sounds so like the language of the sailor folk, a language which I cannot understand.

T sometimes so befalls that, when a storm is raging, down among the slippery beach boulders creep the fisher munes to gather rope and corks for purposes unknown as well to me as you—and never by my magic yet have I at all prevailed to find the secret of this thing they do. But both the king and I witness day by day how boldly they do argue, for the mere possession of the corks and rope, with munes sea-washed and often green.

"AND as once day an elephant I made, to set the island folk a task of hunting, so was I stared at by a party of eight, no more, no less, that I saw them, upright, as it were a picture set on one end; and so it was thus and thus until——

"THE elephant appeared within a wood of oblong shape, again like all the rest before, and I ordained that three munes should hunt him night and day, so to work upon this nervous elephant at each attack that he, in trumpeting his woes, would thus disclose those secrets which I yearned to know.

"AND then came I to where my magic grave place to science; and peradventure created I a shell, a common conch, and it was given to a small mune charge over this shell to give and take fair messages, all unseen though heard afar, much like the throb of electrics sound throughout the world, and all munes came around about and this conch-shell worshipped, leaving me no wiser than before as to the meaning of the messages which came and went and came and went again.

"**A**ND because of this I was wroth and sent among them fires of grass and of peat, but ere it burned these worshippers there came upon it the immunes, which I then had clean forgot, and worked a magic of their own all unbeknown to me, of simply protesting hands which chilled my magic spell and sent my flames hurtling back from whence they came and all but me destroying in their angry heat and hate.

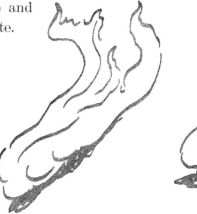

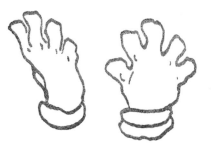

"NOW, having by my own forethought so contrived to divert suspicion from myself concerning certain magic weaknesses, and having thus created the lone wolf at Wolf Corner for to divert the munes from my own magic and to cause them to think of something else, I sat me down for to ponder awhile; and as I pondered I fell asleep, perchance to dream away this power from the munes, and as I dreamed thusly and thusly, arranging a little here and adjusting a little there, I fancied I myself was somewhat of a mune, for certain it was that I was small and of a goodly toughness—and I bristled much in small, hard points like munes oft have upon their persons. And as I studied these excrescences I saw myself reflected in a pool filled full of creatures all with waving, flower-like arms, anemones, they say, and all my sharp points seemed to lengthen and to narrow, and right soon I found me no arms nor legs wherewith to walk or move; but so crept I in between those waving anemone arms within my own reflection, that now I saw that I must be like them, a creature of the sea; and soon did I discover that quite round and flattened had I become with myriad spines forthwith protruding, each independent of his fellow, an urchin of the sea; and as I crept within this glistening salt sea-pool, came to its rim much people; all were munes of my own creation, mariner and fisher munes, and looked at me

and dipped for me with hands and forks and nets; and much seaweed did they gather in, but never me. For in a crevice did I lay, and stiffened all my spines to hold, perchance, should they with stick or knife try to wrench me from my hiding. So I dreamed; but as I lay I dreamed again within my dream and again was I him who had created munes by magic.

"AND my magic ere it spent itself returned, and now I waked and looked and stretched and spat, for much seawater was caught up within that dream, and, looking, I was wont to make a new and godly creature come upon this island him whom I dubbed the unmolested, for though mine were subject to molest, yet the unsettled went and came and went again. And in this unmolested one place I my future hopes of learning more about the secrets of the mines."

And here the wizard paused to take his breath. He breathed a lot and told a lot, well-nigh exhausting not so much his magic as the other thing you know. "And now," quoth he, "I'll rest me by whiles," for to make good progress was he bent, such progress toward getting of his gat—and gat, you know, means much.

So, while the unmolested stood and stood again, and in his striding most of the island covered, like unto the knight's move on the chess-board, while the other pieces slept the wizard rested up. And so the unmolested stood and stood again and naught therefore befell until

AND then the wizard waked from out his lethargy and stretched and wiped his eyes and looked and kenned, and as he kenned what had befallen his own created kingdom's knight he repented him of the new creation of the unmolested, and he spake and said: "Now am I wroth, indeed; I shall therefore unthrone the bold usurper, and him will I cause to wander, unmolested, yet fearful always of an unknown dread." And when he had thus planned the unmolested from the king's throne spake, and "Nothing doing" was the comment which he made. At which the wizard stared and, like the bee honey in the comb, the nectar in the flower, the dewdrop on the body of the stinging bee, he soft and with fair, smooth, persuasive words of hidden magic spake, and this he said:

"Thus and thus, my unmolested one, you speak, and thus you think, for I have made you thus, and thus you are and thus you will remain, and 'Nothing doing' is the word which you shall always use whenever you speak, for I ordain it so."

"And yet," the unmolested said, "and yet."

"And yet," the wizard here replied, scratching his black hairs, sore to gain, perchance, a new and welcome thought.

"And then, what next, my boy?" the unmolested ventured to reply.

"See here, my friend, let us, you and I, have

done," the wizard cried, losing all his self-control, for never had any of his best creations ever spoken thus.

"It seems the thing for you to do, O wizard, is to just dry up and hidden not my reign, for reign I must and shall; and I shall from my throne dictate to all the runes, for, unlike him whom I deposed, I am what I am, unmolested and undone, and very wise, and you a very fool to stand there gaping while I think."

Thus came the overwhelming full rebuff the wizard to withstand was all but baffled, yet one little thing saved his utter ruin - his magic.

AND he spake again, turning his back and wide cloak to shut out that unwelcome sight, an own creation with rebellion fraught, and to himself he spake and said this much:

"If by fair words or overruling I can naught prevail, I will take unto me all my munes, and we will hold a thing, like any Norseman's clan, and I shall gather in all the knowledge I instilled into their brains and I will hurl it at that unmolested head, till, wild with continuous assault, he will dodge and try to hide beneath his throne, where I shall cause the island dogs to lurk and fall upon him to devour— but no, I'm wrong, that's not the way; for I have caused him unmolested for to be, and there's the rub; whether it is best to be or not to be, and not to be is best if he's to fall. And if no other plan occur, to hurl this mad creation from that throne; then will I cause a thought to come within his mind. He shall suddenly of great curiosity overwhelmed be, and, like those other munes who, all unknowing, fell into the sea, he'll flee the throne and make the plunge to know what ever has befallen him whom he deposed; and as he is about to plunge, lo! the mist wraiths they will take him up, and he shall sail away still unmolested and content, thinking he still is king. And I shall forthwith wade and scramble out among the slippery rocks and gather in and still shall gather in all until I come to that first king whose eyes alone are worth a kingdom's ransom.

"And he shall once more sit upon his throne of roots and silent be, and all his rougher parts like unto an egg in smoothness shall become washed as they have been by the sea.

 "THEREFORE will proceed with a calm assurance to again create, and now I'll make one a dancing one, one who will dance for those who wish to see, and he shall dance and dance and dance until the cows come home, which cows will I also thus create to serve a double purpose: home to come and milk to give; and all the men shall hereafter wax fat with milk and the cows stay lean with home-coming o'er the rough brooks from the pastures on the heights above.

"AND every time they return home the dancing mune will cease his tango steps and squat like any savage African to rest through milking time. And he, forced to dance always until the cows return, would beg these lean kine on his bended knees to linger ere they went upon their outward rugged uptrending way to perch upon the pinnacle of the rocky heights and gather moss for fodder; but these kine, though kindly they would listen to his wail, could not be stayed, for wizard magic held them, home to come and milk to give."

BUT so it came about that as the munes full fat betime were grown, so with much efficiency was swelled the head of him that sly magician who, now that ease was stealing over the island, forthwith created him another being, this a monstrous ant, saying: "Now shall I my ant create, to feed upon their munish fat, for sure it is a state of lethargy will steal upon them ere they're done with drinking milk, if these calories are allowed to be imbibed." And straightway there stood the ant, gaunt and thin, newly created, a fulfilment of the wizard's magic schemes—an empty, graven image, but of godly cavernous gorge ready to imbibe the calories from fattening munes.

And here in spite of magic boldness, did the wizard quail and tremble. He had never, in his wildest dream of how the ant would get the calories from fatted munes, seen happenings which he equalled in their wildness these wild scenes which then ensued and over which the totoms had to draw a veil.

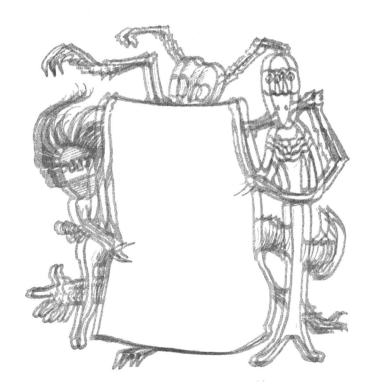

OW, with the munes reduced again to slimness and the ant grown fat with calories was a new difficulty presented, of reversed conditions. Once more spake the wizard loud and clear for all to understand the portent of that word he spoke, and he spake thus:

"It pleases me to see that all is normal far and near, the munes reduced, my ant made fat with these good calories she loves so well, so I ordain that she shall be a pussy cat unto the driftwood king, for driftwood king he's dubbed from now forevermore, and she my ant shall sit upon the topmost stump of the king's throne and purr like any cat can do if only she doth will, and thus shall a new musician added be to him who is your king, you know, for so thus have I made my will to be. And should a mune or two grow saucy and of the king make sport, as is the wont of social munes and such, then will my ant thrust out and grab them by the hinder parts and forthwith fling them out to sea, for to be ground as is the wont of all who therein plunge, and thus shall my king and my good new created and caloried ant be friends indeed, and I may make her queen for aught I now can tell.

"Now, to that knowledge which I planned for all my munes at their great meeting called a thing, I shall add all the calories my ant has eat to strengthen up the secret knowledge stored within my nut—and great and mighty works unwrought as yet I'll do with these my nutty thoughts." And, speaking thus, with great conceit he winked an eye, and then another eye, and still another eye, for he could boast of having many eyes beneath his wizard garb quite hard and glassy, and when ere he budged they clinked like agates, pewees, and the rest, the sort of marbles urchins not of sea but land do carry at a certain time of year wherewith to play.

S placed the eyeballs in a magic circle, for to wink at that great spell he fain would cast about a spot whereon the munes had set the nervous elephant to be the better hunted openly all night and day, deeming the dark, thick wood of fold and twisted roots and stumps no place for munes to hunt, leastwise the nervous elephant.

And now to show you how this spell the wizard cast, I'll just repeat the things he said forth as he spake:

"All empty teeth, all empty nuts, all empty pods, beware! for I your wizard have withdrawn therefrom the contents of that great gray tissue which in munes is sawdust eaten by the little ants, and here mix I into it clorides one, two, and three, in dozens and in pints and quarts, as doth a milkman measure up his milk and water store. Oh goodly ant of mine, deliver up your clorides and be a midden pussy catted ant to him thy king.

"Oh, sawdust, from the munish tissue gray from out these empty headed munes form in piles before the nervous one, who in his trunk will take you up and squirt you twixt my magic spell and me, to make a sort of atmosphere through which no mune nor immune ere can penetrate.

"All seeing eyes, in circles as you lay, wink at all this, and observe how winking without eyelids, yet you wink, and just observe me as I will create out of this magic spell a thing, a nameless thing, the nameless one, so cunning and so sly that even he called Sherlock Holmes could not prevail through his deductions and a name for it could find."

ND hardly had the wizard spoken thus until all marvelled; then up started all the munes and creatures of his own creation for to come around and mob him, lest he by his new-discovered magic all most utterly destroy. And they kept in a ring round him and his magic ring, the lone wolf and the dogs of hunting and of biting, too, the eight who stared at you and me like anything, the king and all his four or five musicians, all thumping, pounding, scraping, piping, and the like, and the ant, now gaunt and thin as nature made her in her first created state, and all the immunes with protesting hands; also the fisher munes come inshore just for once to see what this great fuss was all about, and him that tiny mune still bearing in his arms the sacred conch, and all the munes who worshipped at that conkish shrine. They who sat around at close of day and gossiped while the wizard spied them out. All the torch-birds, ten or more or less, one could not count their number as they flew and fanned away the fiery flames they carried to show what they had been made to do. All these and many more did their own particular stunt, as they gathered in a great mass, met together as *the clan of munes*, to judge the wizard and to use him and his totems, his Indian finery, his house and his canoe and everything which he possessed in one great potlatch spree, once and for all to rid them of the great and magic stunt which he had planned to do. They would take no more risks from magic other than their own, for all had greatly feared that nameless thing he said he would create, and they were tired of his magic tricks.

So when the disappointed little totem rattles gathered up and scuttled off with all the magic eyeballs which were clean forgot, a situation arose between the wizard and the munes that beggars all description. No pictures, words, or any other means could tell you just what the situation really had become.

Printed in the USA
CPSIA information can be obtained
at www.ICGtesting.com
LVHW071031130823

755077LV00004B/27